My Home Country

PERU

IS MY HOME

For a free color catalog describing Gareth Stevens' list of high-quality books, call 1-800-341-3569 (USA) or 1-800-461-9120 (Canada).

For their help in the preparation of *My Home Country: Peru Is My Home*, the editors gratefully acknowledge the help of Assistant US Secretary of State Betty Tamposi; US Consul General Wayne Griffith; Norma Cobacha; James Blanford of the US State Department Bureau of Consular Affairs; Frank Sibley; American Airlines, which generously provided transportation; and Dora Diaz of Mount Mary College, Milwaukee, Wisconsin.

Flag illustration on page 42, © Flag Research Center

Library of Congress Cataloging-in-Publication Data

Karpfinger, Beth.
    Peru is my home / adapted from Barbara Radcliffe Rogers' Children of the world—Peru by Beth Karpfinger ; photographs by Stillman Rogers.
       p. cm. — (My home country)
    Includes bibliographical references and index.
    Summary: A look at the life of a twelve-year-old girl and her family living in Lima. Includes a section with information on Peru.
    ISBN 0-8368-0903-3
    1. Peru—Social life and customs—Juvenile literature. [1. Family life—Peru. 2. Peru.] I. Rogers, Stillman, 1939- ill. II. Rogers, Barbara Radcliffe. Peru. III. Title. IV. Series.
F3410.K37 -1993
985—dc20
                                                    92-30685

Edited, designed, and produced by

Gareth Stevens Publishing
1555 North RiverCenter Drive, Suite 201
Milwaukee, Wisconsin 53212, USA

Text, photographs, and format copyright 1993 by Gareth Stevens, Inc. First published in the United States and Canada in 1993 by Gareth Stevens, Inc. This US edition is abridged from *Children of the World: Peru*, copyright 1992 by Gareth Stevens, Inc., with text by Barbara Radcliffe Rogers and photographs by Stillman Rogers.

Series editors: Barbara J. Behm and Beth Karpfinger
Research editor: Chandrika Kaul, Ph.D.
Cover design: Kristi Ludwig
Designer: Beth Karpfinger
Map design: Sheri Gibbs

Printed in the United States of America

1 2 3 4 5 6 7 8 9 96 95 94 93

My Home Country

PERU
IS MY HOME

Adapted from Barbara Radcliffe Rogers'
Children of the World: Peru

by Beth Karpfinger
Photographs by Stillman Rogers

Gareth Stevens Publishing
MILWAUKEE

Twelve-year-old Anna Patricia Martinez, known as Patita, lives with her extended family in Lima, Peru's seaside capital. Although her own father is dead, the men in her extended family act as substitute fathers, and her best friends are her family. While attending one of the best schools in Lima, Patita learns fascinating details about her country's colorful past. Aided by her brother, she also becomes proficient on the computer.

To enhance this book's value in libraries and classrooms, clear and simple reference sections include up-to-date information about Peru's history, land and climate, people and language, education, and religion. *Peru Is My Home* also features a large and colorful map, bibliography, glossary, simple index, research topics, and activity projects designed especially for young readers.

The living conditions and experiences of children in Peru vary according to economic, environmental, and ethnic circumstances. The reference sections help bring to life for young readers the diversity and richness of the culture and heritage of Peru. Of particular interest are discussions of the powerful Inca empire that once ruled all of Peru and much of South America and the country's current economic and political woes.

My Home Country includes the following titles:

Canada	*Nicaragua*
Costa Rica	*Peru*
Cuba	*Poland*
El Salvador	*South Africa*
Guatemala	*Vietnam*
Ireland	*Zambia*

CONTENTS

LIVING IN PERU:
Anna Patricia, a Serious Student

Anna Patricia Martinez is a 12-year-old girl from Peru. Her home is in Jesús María, a part of Peru's capital city of Lima.

Anna Patricia lives with her mother, her brother, and her mother's parents. Because Anna Patricia has the same first name as her mother, she is called Patita.

Patita and her mother say, "Hello." *"Buenas dias!"* ▶

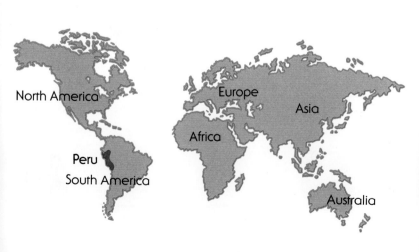

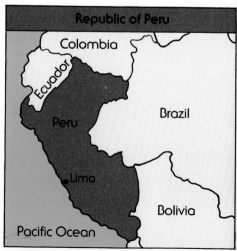

Lima has many public parks and squares with benches so people can sit and enjoy the gardens and shade trees.

Living in Lima

Lima is a very big city and a very old one. Many of its buildings, especially the churches, were built over 400 years ago.

Patita's neighborhood is one of Lima's newer ones. The streets are wide, and the homes are made of brick. Almost all of the houses have tiny front yards with flowering bushes.

Many Indian families from the Andes Mountains of Peru move to the city of Lima. Since housing in the city is limited, they build houses on empty lots, using whatever materials they can find. These *pueblos jovenes*, or young villages, have no electricity or running water. They are very primitive as well as crowded.

Opposite, top: Many of the homes in Patita's neighborhood have several apartments belonging to different generations of the same family. Opposite, bottom: Indians who have moved into Lima from the mountains often sell food, cooking it right on the street.

The Family Sticks Together

When Patita was six years old, her father died from cancer. Without the income from his job, Patita's family could not afford a house of their own. So they moved into Patita's grandparents' home.

Patita's aunt and uncle live next door with their two grown daughters. When another aunt and uncle could not afford to own a home, Patita's grandparents helped them build a third-story addition onto the house next door.

Patita's aunts and cousins feel right at home in her grandparents' house.

The homes of all of Patita's relatives are like a small neighborhood. Although each is a separate apartment, they all connect in the backyard. Yards like these are very common in South America.

The grandparents' house is home to everyone — aunts, uncles, and cousins. They all stop by to visit or join in a meal.

◀ **Rooms have been added on top of this home to make more living space for the family.**

Patita's favorite place is next to her grandfather's chair.

Family and Friends —
One and the Same

Patita's older brother is named Enrique. Enrique is mildly mentally retarded. Peru has no special schools for students with special needs, but his family and teachers have helped him finish high school.

Enrique uses his computer to type papers for students.

Carlita and Patita pretend their dolls are going to fancy parties.

Enrique is very good at using a computer. He also teaches Patita how to work with it.

Patita often spends time with her best friend and cousin, Carlita. Because the cousins live next to each other, they can play together whenever they want.

A Rush to School

On school days, Patita wakes up at 7:00 a.m., eats her breakfast, and puts on her school uniform.

"Hurry, Carlita!" she calls to her cousin up the stairs. Patita picks up her books and meets Carlita for the walk to school. School is a 20-minute walk from home.

School begins at 8:00 a.m. Patita gets a yellow smock from her locker and puts it on over her uniform. Each grade has a certain color smock.

Opposite, top: Smocks are worn over the school uniforms.
Opposite, bottom: The Maria Alvarado School was built in 1906.
Above: Each grade level is assigned a certain color smock.

Anna Patricia's class picture.

Maria Alvarado School — A Family Tradition

The Maria Alvarado School was founded in 1906 by missionaries from the United States. Patita's mother and most of her cousins attended this same school.

The school is big. It has three separate courtyards. One courtyard looks like a park.

The hallways open out onto these courtyards, which helps keep the school bright and cool.

The school offers six years of elementary school and five years of high school — grades seven through eleven.

Left: Art students set their easels in the open corridor. Below: Patita's classmates listen carefully to the teacher.

The first class of the morning is science, then math, Spanish language and literature, social studies, and English. English is Patita's favorite subject.

After fifth period, everyone goes out into the courtyard for lunch. Most of the students bring their lunches from home. They buy drinks from a counter in the school yard. Patita has different kinds of fruits and vegetables for lunch.

Her teacher watches as Patita writes on the blackboard.

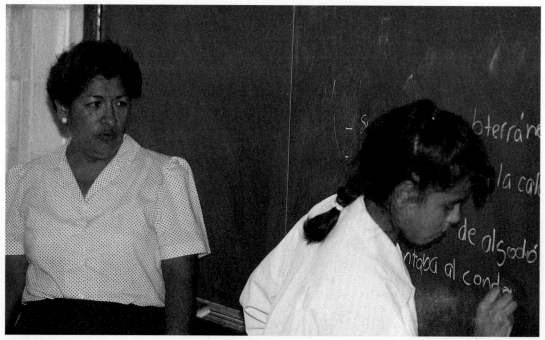

The girls sit in circles in the
school yard at lunchtime.

Students can buy drinks from a
snack bar in the school yard.

Because Lima's climate is so mild, flowers bloom all year and grow to be quite large.

At the Maria Alvarado School, each student must learn how to use a computer as well as a typewriter.

Patita is a very serious and dedicated student and always finishes her work on time. All her teachers expect that she will be accepted at a university. She will be able to choose from a variety of careers that interest her, since women in Peru have greater opportunities than ever before.

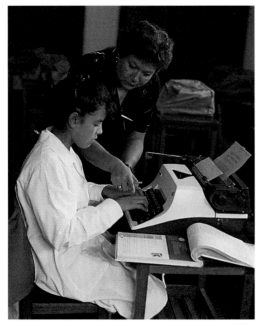

Top: Her teacher is pleased that Patita is able to practice on a computer at home as well as at school.

Bottom: Typing is a required course for all students.

25

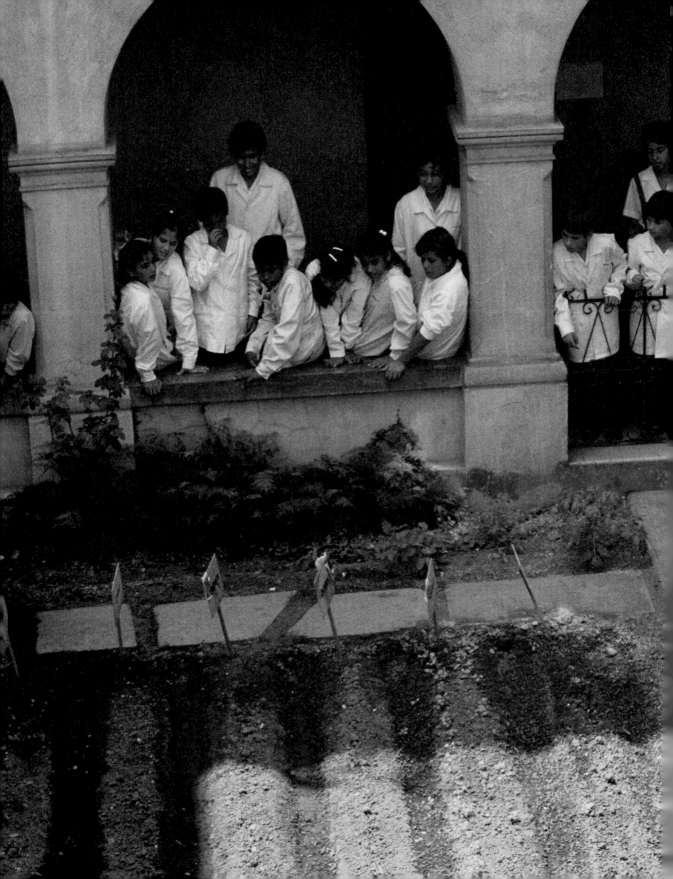

In addition to the usual subjects, Maria Alvarado School offers gardening classes. One courtyard has garden beds for growing fruits, vegetables, and herbs.

Patita often studies in the school library during her lunch hour.

Left: One class teaches students how to grow food in a garden. Below: Patita checks out books from the school library.

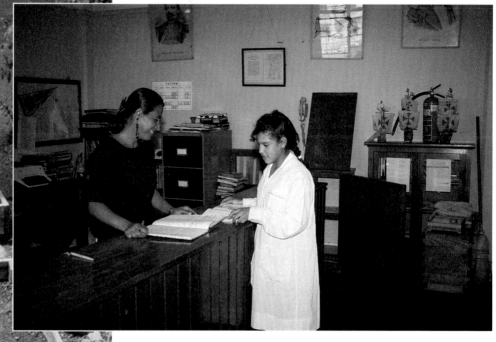

People of the early civilizations of Peru often made their pottery
in the shapes of fanciful animals and birds.

Learning about Peru's History

Patita and her friends like to look at pottery made in Peru over 1,000 years ago. They are studying Peru's history in social studies class.

Patita has never visited Cuzco, the mountain city where Inca Indians lived 500 years ago. Along the mountainsides, Indians still raise corn and potatoes. They use foot plows and short hand hoes, just as the Incas did long ago.

Left, top: This woman is weaving a complicated design. Left, bottom: Women can spin wool as they walk, even on rough, uneven trails.

Although the Incas did not use wheels or animals to move stones up the mountains, they were able to build huge stone walls there. Their stonecutters were so expert that, even today, a knife blade cannot be slipped between the stones.

Herds of llamas graze in the mountain villages near Cuzco. Women who live there still spin wool into yarn on hand spindles. Life in these villages is very different from Patita's modern neighborhood.

Thatch made of grass or leaves is a common roofing material in the mountain villages near Cuzco.

Both llamas and alpacas provide wool for clothing and blankets. Inset: An Indian woman separates wool fibers so she can spin the wool into yarn. Her spindle is set up in front of her.

Only ruins remain of the ancient Inca city of Machu Picchu.

After School

Patita looks forward to eating a snack after school. She eats a piece of *Pastelle de Manzanas.* This is like apple pie, but the crust is sweeter, almost like a sugar cookie.

Patita often studies throughout the evening, stopping only to do chores and eat with her family. If there is time left over, she may play with her cousin for a little while.

Patita studies on the patio. ▸
Below: Patita studies English and the history of the Incas.

Above: Patita's cousins often eat
at their grandparents' house.
Inset: Patita likes the way her
mother prepares chicken and rice.

Dinner with Patita's Family

Patita and her mother usually cook dinner
together in the evenings. Each meal begins
with a salad and is followed by homemade

soup and the main course. Patita's favorite foods are chicken and rice or the Chinese dishes her mother sometimes prepares.

The family's big kitchen table always seems crowded. Unless Patita stays at her aunt's to have dinner with Carlita, she and her family have meals together. At dinner, each person tells about her or his day, and stories and laughter soon fill the air.

"I think the rice is ready," Patita tells her mother as she carefully stirs the pot.

Markets in Peru

Patita's mother does her shopping on Saturday mornings. She shops at the local open-air market. There, farm families gather every weekend to sell vegetables, fruits, and meat that they have grown on their farms.

Nearby, sidewalk vendors sell small items in baskets or from little pushcarts.

Top: Spaniards first brought potatoes to Europe from Peru. Bottom: Indians carry produce to market in large baskets or in shawls tied to their backs.

Shoppers in Lima welcome fresh-picked fruits and vegetables.

Also near the open-air markets, Indians sell their handiwork such as pottery, baskets, embroidery, and their knitting and weaving.

Relaxing on the Weekend

After a busy week, the weekend is a time for relaxing. In warm weather, all the family members get together to spend at least one day of each weekend at the beach.

Whenever one of Patita's classmates has a birthday, a celebration is held on a Saturday night. The entire class is invited to the classmate's home for conversation, laughter, pizza, and dancing to the music on the radio.

Patita and her class get together on Saturday nights each time a classmate celebrates a birthday.

MORE FACTS ABOUT: Peru

Official Name: República del Peru
(ray-POO-blee-kah
del PAY-roo)
Republic of Peru

Capital: Lima

History

The earliest major civilization in Peru was the
Chavin culture in 850 B.C. At the beginning of the
13th century, a people near Lake Titicaca formed
one of the world's greatest empires — Inca. In
1532, a Spanish soldier named Francisco Pizarro
conquered the Incas, and Peru remained under
Spain's rule until the early 19th century.

In 1845, Ramón Castilla became president of Peru.
His government built schools, railroads, and
telegraph lines that drew the country together.
But it wasn't until 1980 that a president was
chosen in a free election. In 1990, Alberto
Fujimori was elected president. He is currently
trying to rid Peru of a huge debt caused by the
years of military rule.

Land and Climate

The Pacific Ocean forms the western border of Peru. Immediately east of the Pacific coast are the Andes Mountains. Scattered throughout the Andes are grassy highland plains, the largest part being the Amazon rain forest. The climate along the coast is hot and dry; the area east of the Andes is tropical.

People and Language

Forty-six percent of Peru's population is of pure Indian ancestry. *Mestizos*, people with mixed Spanish and Indian blood, make up about 38 percent of the population. Both Spanish and Quechua (the language of the Incas) are the official languages of Peru.

Education

All children between the ages of seven and sixteen are required to attend elementary school. Elementary classes are free. Secondary education is also free, but students are not required to attend.

The units of currency used in Peru are called Intis.

Religion

Nearly 90 percent of Peruvians are Catholic, but many of these are Indians who combine the beliefs of the Catholic faith with the customs and traditions of their native faiths. Many Indian Christians also worship Inca gods.

Sports and Recreation

Soccer is the national sport. In Peru, however, it is called *fútbol* (football). Street soccer is played with whatever type of ball is available. Lima's National Stadium is decorated with painted laurel wreaths showing the names of Peru's best-loved athletes. About half of the sports stars named are women.

Peruvians in North America

There are no large concentrations of immigrants from Peru in North America. However, there has been a recent wave of immigration of an unusual kind. North American families are adopting Peruvian babies orphaned by poverty, disease, or terrorist attacks on their families. Nearly every airline flight between Lima, Peru, and the United States carries several Peruvian infants moving north to begin a new life with their adoptive parents.

Glossary of Useful Spanish Terms

adios (ah-dee-OHS): goodbye

ola (OH-lah): hello

Glossary of Useful Quechua Terms

ari (ah-REE): yes

mana (MAH-nah): no

More Books about Peru

A Family in Peru. St. John (Lerner Publications)
Peru. (Chelsea House)
Peru in Pictures. Staff (Lerner Publications)

Things To Do

1. For a Peruvian pen pal, write to: Worldwide Pen Friends, P.O. Box 39097, Downey, CA 90241. Be sure to tell them what country you want your pen pal to be from. Also include your full name, age, and address.

2. If you could meet Patita in person, what questions would you ask her about Peru, her school, and her family? What would you tell her about your country, the school that you attend, and your family?

PERU – Political and Physical

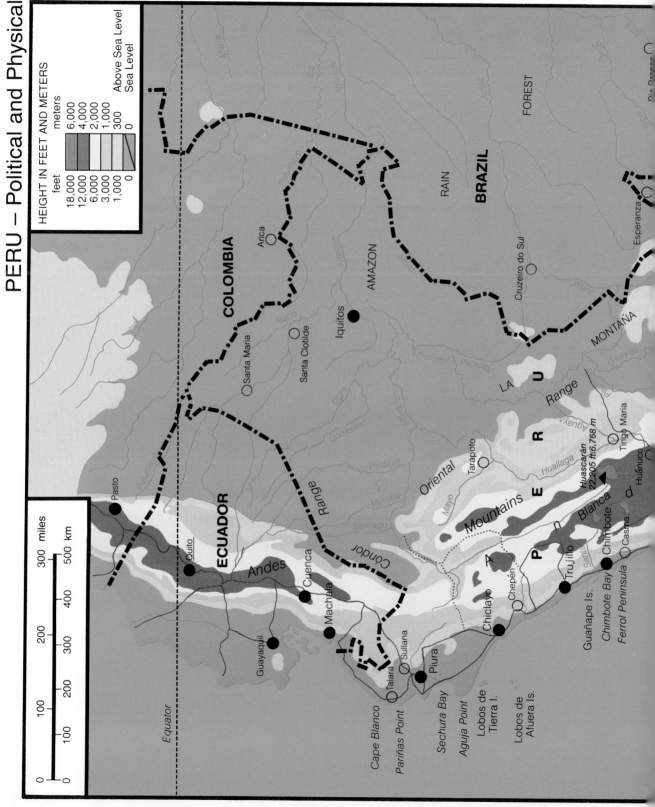

HEIGHT IN FEET AND METERS

feet	meters
18,000	6,000
12,000	4,000
6,000	2,000
3,000	1,000
1,000	300
0	0

Above Sea Level

Sea Level

COLOMBIA

ECUADOR

BRAZIL

PERU

AMAZON

RAIN

FOREST

Pasto

Quito

Cuenca

Machala

Guayaquil

Andes

Talara

Cape Blanco

Pariñas Point

Sullana

Piura

Sechura Bay

Aguja Point

Lobos de Tierra I.

Lobos de Afuera Is.

Chiclayo

Chepén

Trujillo

Chimbote

Casma

Guañape Is.

Chimbote Bay

Ferrol Peninsula

Huánuco

Tingo Maria

Tarapoto

Huascarán 22,205 ft/6,768 m

Cordillera Blanca

Mountains

Oriental

Condor Range

Range

Santa Maria

Santa Clotilde

Iquitos

Arica

Cruzeiro do Sul

Esperanza

MONTAÑA

LA

Equator

0   100   200   300 miles

0   100   200   300   400   500 km

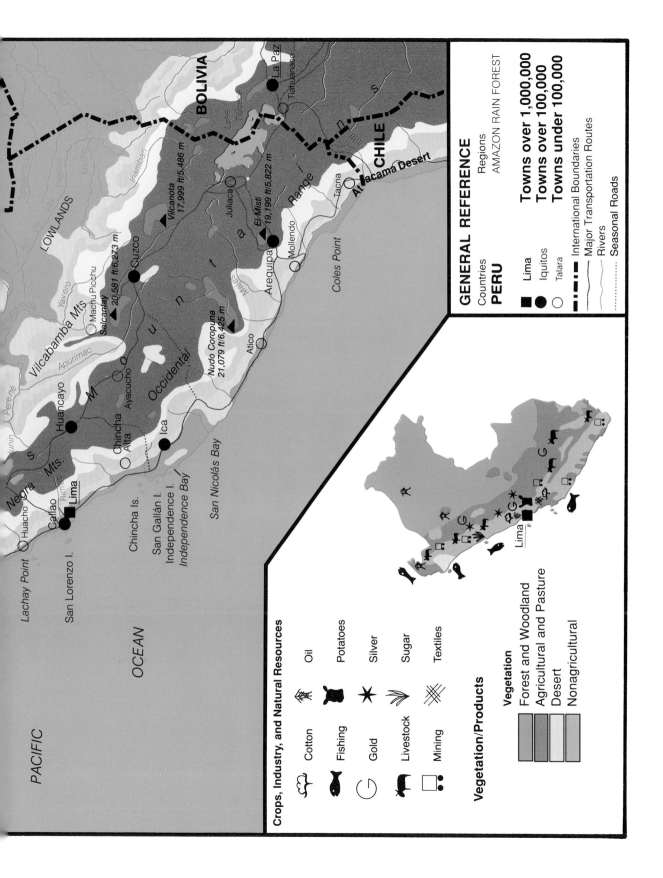

PACIFIC

OCEAN

Lachay Point

San Lorenzo I.

Huacho ○
Callao ●
Lima ■
Rímac

Chincha Is.

San Gallán I.
Independence I.
Independence Bay

San Nicolás Bay

Coles Point

Machu Picchu ○
Salcantay
▲ 20,581 ft/6,273 m

Vilcabamba Mts.

Apurímac

Yavero

Río de la

Urubamba

Cuzco ●

Huancayo ●

Chincha
Alta ○

Ica ●

Ayacucho ○

Negra
Mts.

Junín

Perene

Mantaro

LOWLANDS

Río de las Piedres

Tahuamanu

Madre

Inambari

Vilcanota
17,999 ft/5,486 m ▲

Juliaca ○

El Misti
19,199 ft/5,822 m ▲

Arequipa ●

Mollendo ○

Nudo Coropuna
21,079 ft/6,425 m ▲

Atico ○

Matas

Occidental

Mtn.

t

a

R
a
n
g
e

A
n
d
e
s

BOLIVIA

La Paz ●
Tiahuanaco ○

Lake
Titicaca

Desaguadero

Tacna ○

CHILE

Atacama Desert

GENERAL REFERENCE

Countries
PERU

Regions
AMAZON RAIN FOREST

■ Lima   **Towns over 1,000,000**
● Iquitos   **Towns over 100,000**
○ Talara   **Towns under 100,000**

▬ ▬ International Boundaries
——— Major Transportation Routes
——— Rivers
·········· Seasonal Roads

Crops, Industry, and Natural Resources

🐑 Cotton   🐟 Oil

🐋 Fishing   🥔 Potatoes

Ⓖ Gold   ✴ Silver

🐄 Livestock   🌾 Sugar

▫ Mining   🗺 Textiles

Vegetation/Products

Vegetation

Forest and Woodland

Agricultural and Pasture

Desert

Nonagricultural

Lima

Index